TIME WARP TRIO™

Time Warp Trio™ is produced by WGBH in association with Soup2Nuts for Discovery Kids.

HarperTrophy® is a registered trademark of HarperCollins Publishers.

Time Warp Trio®
Time Warp Trio: You Can't, but Genghis Khan
Copyright © 2006 WGBH Educational Foundation and Chucklebait, Inc.
Artwork, Designs and Animation © 2005 WGBH Educational Foundation.
Library of Congress catalog card number: 2006924550
ISBN-10: 0-06-111636-X — ISBN-13: 978-0-06-111636-0

Typography by Joe Merkel
❖
First Harper Trophy edition, 2006

TIME WARP TRIO ™

YOU CAN'T, BUT GENGHIS KHAN

Time Warp Trio created by
Jon Scieszka
Adapted by
Jennifer Frantz
Adapted from the teleplay by
Steve Granat and Cydne Clark

HarperTrophy®
An Imprint of HarperCollins Publishers

CHAPTER 1

"**G**et off me, you overgrown lamb chop!" Fred yelled. He was on the ground, pinned beneath a sheep that was lapping at his face like a snow cone.

Meanwhile, Sam was struggling with another giant puffball. "Go away," he said. "I'm allergic to wool." Which is true, but then again what *isn't* Sam allergic to?

I looked around, trying to figure out where we'd ended up this time, but other than the kissing sheep, there weren't too many clues.

Mountains. Grass. Sheep. Sheep. Grass. Mountains.

Yep, that was about it.

"Where are we?" I asked Sam and Fred, who had broken free of their woolly new best friends.

"We're nowhere," Fred said, eyeing the grassy landscape. "It's like . . . Outer Mongolia or something!"

"I don't see a single thing besides grass," Sam added. "Maybe over . . . *AAAAAAAAH*!"

Sam was suddenly face-to-face with a man in a pointed cap and a weird outfit trimmed with fur. Sam was still trying to catch his breath when the man's tan face lit up with a big, gummy smile. Wherever we were, people were not big on flossing—

but, hey, at least they were friendly.

"Where'd he come from?" I asked, looking around.

"That's a yurt," Sam said, pointing to our friend's big round home. "It's a tent used by nomads in . . . in . . . Outer Mongolia."

Outer Mongolia. Just our luck. Weird stuff is always happening to us, especially when *The Book* is involved. Speaking of *The Book*, we'd have to find it before we could get out of this sheepy, grassy nowhereland and back to Brooklyn, New York. We always seemed to lose *The Book* when we warped, and, judging from the look of our surroundings, this time was no different.

I noticed our new nomadic pal had a cart parked near his yurt. "Uh, sir," I said. "Could we hitch a ride with you to, say, Inner Mongolia?"

That didn't seem to get through to him. He just stared at me blankly. So Fred decided to translate using his best caveman imitation.

"Me—Fred," he grunted. "You—" But before Fred could finish, the nomad leaned closer and started sniffing him.

"I think it's some sort of Mongolian greeting," Sam suggested.

As quickly as it started, the sniffing stopped. The nomad suddenly looked like he'd seen a ghost. He pointed a shaky hand behind us. We turned around to find out what could be so frightening, but all that was there was a big cloud of dust. Mountains. Grass. Sheep. *And* dust. Outer Mongolia was turning out to be one exciting place. . . .

Sam squinted through his glasses in the direction the nomad pointed. Then he asked, "What's he pointing at?"

We turned back and our nomad pal was gone—cart, yurt, and all.

"That's weird," Fred said. "I wonder what got into him."

"Uh…guys…" Sam gasped. "I think I know."

Fred and I turned around again and looked. The giant dust cloud had settled, and in its place was a band of ferocious Mongolian warriors on horseback.

"I'm guessing that's not the Mongolian polo team," I said. And I was right.

CHAPTER 2

*O*kay. Before we become Mongolian road-kill, I should explain how we got into this mess. Like most of our time-warp adventures, this one started in a really weird way—with take-out menus.

It was just a typical day at my house in Brooklyn. We were hanging out in the kitchen, and Sam was flipping through some take-out menus trying to decide on something for us to eat.

"How about we get Mexican food?" Sam suggested. "Joe, you like chimichangas, right?"

Fred and I didn't hear a word Sam said. We were concentrating on more important matters.

"One Digital Demon is worth TEN Phlegm Monsters," I snapped at Fred.

"Are you serious?" Fred fired back. "The Phlegm Monster can hurl a loogie through solid steel! Not even the Dark Lord can fight that."

"Pizza? Pizza's good," Sam said to no one in particular. "Or how about this—Khan's Mongolian Barbeque?"

I was starting to get a little hungry, but I had to put Fred in his place about the Phlegm Monster's loogie-hurling talent. "*That*," I said, "was before the Dark Lord split into Octopus Man and Tina the Waitress. Now he's immune to bodily fluids."

By this point, Sam was annoyed. He got up and threw the take-out menus back in a drawer and slammed it shut. "Fine," he said. "You can starve for all I—"

But Sam's freak-out was interrupted by the

kitchen drawer flying open and spewing out a wispy line of familiar green mist. *The Book* was in the drawer!

"What'd you do?" I yelled at Sam. I raced over and grabbed *The Book*. The Mongolian barbecue menu fluttered out of the drawer and onto the floor.

I had to act fast, before the green mist warped us to some strange place. Ever since my uncle gave me *The Book*, it has been nothing but trouble. Every time we open it, it takes us to a different place and time. While that is really cool, there's one problem. *The Book* always disappears, leaving us with no way back to our own time. So I had to think. The green mist whirled closer. I was running out of options. I did what any good magician would do—I made up my very own spell:

"Green mist, go away,
  'Cause here in Brooklyn
  we want to stay."

I could hardly believe it—my spell worked. Fred, Sam, and I looked at each other, shocked and relieved. We'd stopped the green mist before it warped us away to some strange place and time. This was a first.

"What was that?" Sam asked.

"I don't know," I said. "It just seemed like something that might work."

"I can't believe it," said Sam.

Then the three of us looked down. Our eyes grew wide. Our bottom halves had already disappeared.

"Well," said Fred. "Let's say it half-worked."

The green mist swirled up over the rest of us. There was no stopping the magic of *The Book* once it had begun.

Fred, Sam, and I warped out of my kitchen in Brooklyn and into Outer Mongolia—land of mountains, grass, sheep, and fighting-warrior horsemen.

And I think we said something like: "WAAAAAAAAAHHH!"

CHAPTER 3

So we learned one time-warp lesson: If you mix *The Book* with a take-out menu, *you* become the barbeque. Which brings us back to the grassy plains of Outer Mongolia. . . .

Two bands of angry-looking horsemen were bearing down on us fast from opposite directions, and there was no place to hide for miles. Looking this way and that, Fred, Sam, and I stumbled backward into each other. Things were not looking good.

Just then, a black shadow fell over us. We looked up and saw a giant black stallion rearing

up, his rider towering high on his back. The stallion's huge body blocked out the sun as the beast let out a snort. I knew we were all wondering the same thing: Was the Time Warp Trio about to become time-warp toast?

Above the sounds of battle, we heard a voice yell, "Climb on!"

A hand reached down and lifted Fred, Sam, and me up onto the back of the huge stallion. We got a good look at the rider, who was now only inches away. He was dressed in some sort of Mongolian battle armor and helmet, but he

couldn't have been much older than us.

"Tchoo!" our rider friend yelled.

I was about to say gesundheit, when I realized it must be some sort of command for his horse. The stallion rocketed forward, hurtling us out of the way just as the two armies of horsemen collided—right in the spot where we'd been standing only moments ago. We'd escaped by seconds. Now that's what I call some fancy *hoof*work.

We had warped right into the middle of a huge fight between two warring tribes. Arrows whizzed overhead. Metal swords clanged against metal swords. These guys meant business. This was a serious grudge match.

Warriors on horseback dodged in and out of the fighting. They fired arrows, swung swords, and turned circles without even having to hold onto their horses.

Horseman fought horseman. Tribe fought tribe. We were in the middle of a real Mongolian beef. And it looked like we were going to be the next ones to be served. . . .

CHAPTER 4

The rider pulled his stallion off into a safe spot behind some boulders. We all dismounted, glad to be alive.

"All right!" Fred shouted, slapping the rider on the back. "We owe you, man!"

That didn't go over too well. In a flash, our new pal drew a very sharp-looking sword from his belt and shoved it in Fred's face. "*No one* strikes a prince of the Borjigid," he said.

A prince. We all stared at the guy. He was just a kid, though he *was* dressed in some pretty fancy battle gear.

Hanging out with a real live Mongolian prince would be pretty cool. Too bad Fred already made him angry. Sunlight glinted off the razor-sharp sword. Sam leaned toward me. "That's a scimitar," he whispered. "It's a curved Asian sword with—"

"I don't care *what* it is," I said. If we didn't turn on the charm, we were going to have a fillet o' Fred on our hands. "Please excuse Fred's manners," I said to the prince. "He was raised by wolves."

"Is this true?" the prince asked with new interest. "I, myself, am descended from the Gray Wolf, and was born with a destiny from heaven on high."

"Oh, yeah?" Fred replied. "Well, *I'm* in Little League." You had to admire Fred's ability to forget he had a scimitar in his face only seconds ago.

The prince narrowed his eyes at Fred. "Really?" he said. "And can you ride two horses at once?"

"Who can't?" said Fred. It was time to raise the stakes. "Can you do *this*?" Fred stuck his hand in his armpit and gave the prince his very best armpit fart.

I guess armpit farts aren't big in ancient Mongolia, because the prince flapped his arm like a sick pigeon and let out a pathetic little squeak.

"I will work on it," he told Fred. He seemed serious.

Since we'd already survived near-death warfare and battle by armpit, I figured it was time for introductions. "So . . . ," I said. "My name's Joe. This is Fred, and that's Sam. We're from the land of Brooklyn."

I stuck my hand out to the prince. He looked at me like I was nuts. Then he started sniffing at it, just like the nomad had sniffed at Fred before. To get the point across, I grabbed the prince's hand and started to shake it.

"It's called a handshake," I explained. "It's a symbol of friendship."

"No sniffing?" he asked. "You *are* strange people."

But I guess he understood, because he shook Fred and Sam's hands, too. Then he introduced himself. "I am Temujin," he said.

"*Temujin*, huh?" Sam said. "Funny, that sounds sorta . . . familiar."

"You have no doubt heard of me," Temujin replied. "My father, Yesugei, is chieftain of our tribe. Look there!"

Temujin leaped up onto a boulder and pointed down to one of the biggest, baddest warriors on the battlefield—his pops.

"See how he leads his army into battle against the Tartar demons!" Temujin added proudly. "He is the bravest man in all of Mongolia!"

"Hmm, Tartars and Mongols battling," said Sam. "This must be the twelfth century, if I remember what was in my history books."

Which reminded me . . .

"Speaking of books," I said to Temujin, "have you seen a blue book with a silver squiggle-thing on the cover?"

"Book?" Temujin asked.

Judging from the look on T.J.'s face, books weren't big in his world. "It's sort of a . . . box, about this big," I said, showing him the size with my hands.

"That sounds familiar," Temujin said. "Yes, I believe I have seen it."

"Great!" Sam squealed. "This is too easy. Where?"

Temujin thought for a moment. "Let me think. . . . Was it . . . ? No . . . Perhaps in the . . . No, it wasn't there."

"Come on," said Fred. "You couldn't miss it. It's the only thing around here that isn't a sheep."

"Maybe you left it in your yurt," I said.

"It *was* somewhere in our camp," Temujin said. "Perhaps I will see it tonight at the victory feast. You will come as my guests."

"*Victory* feast?" I asked. The battle was still raging on below us, with no end in sight. "How do you know your dad is going to win?"

T.J. gave us a big grin. "We ALWAYS win," he said. "We are Borjigid."

CHAPTER 5

Well, there was something to that Borjigid thing after all. Temujin's dad *did* win the battle, and we got to go to the victory feast as T.J.'s special guests.

The feast was held in a huge yurt. We sat on rugs and cushions in a spot of honor, right next to Temujin and his dad. Everyone seemed to be having a good time. There were lots of people and music and food, if you could call it that.

"When did I start chewing this piece of meat?" Sam asked Fred and me between chews. "It was this morning, right?"

"I think my dinner is staring at me," said Fred. There was something that looked like an eyeball floating in his dish.

"What exactly *is* this mystery meat?" I asked Temujin.

"It's mutton, of course," he replied.

Fred wasn't taking any chances. "That's a food, right? Not somebody's name?"

Sam tried to clear his mouth of the sheepy taste by taking a big swig of his drink. Just as he did, Temujin nodded toward Sam's goblet. "That we call koumiss—fermented mare's milk."

"PWAAAAAAAAAAAAAAAH!" Koumiss sprayed out of Sam's mouth like water from a fire hose, soaking a gang of scary-looking warriors seated nearby. One of them had a nasty scar across his face and creepy,

cloudy eyes. I could tell they weren't happy.

The youngest warrior in the gang jumped to his feet and glared at Sam. "You die," he growled.

"Teach him a lesson, Tarkutai!" a boy nearby cheered.

"Stay out of this, Pumlik," the guy named Tarkutai snarled. Then he motioned to the creepy-eyed guy, who raised Sam in the air with one hand and whipped out a dagger with the other.

Temujin leaped up and stared Tarkutai in the eye. "Sam is my guest! He is *not* to be harmed!" Temujin ordered.

After a few tense seconds, Tarkutai backed down. "As you wish . . . my prince," he hissed to T.J.

Tarkutai signaled to his goon Creepy-Eye, who dropped Sam with a thud. Then he headed back to his seat followed by his little brother, Pumlik, and Creepy-Eye.

"Nice guy, in a psycho kind of way," Fred said, after Tarkutai had moved safely out of earshot.

"Tarkutai has long been jealous of my family's position," T.J. explained.

Sam wiped the sweat from his forehead. "And I have long been wanting to find *The Book* and get out of here."

"You mean the blue box you were seeking?" Temujin replied. "I finally remember where I saw it."

Sam jumped upon hearing the good news. "You do? Where?" he asked.

But just as Temujin was about to explain, a girl walked up to us shaking two dice-like things in her hand.

"Hi, Temujin," she said. "Want to play a game of *shagai* later? I'll let you win this time."

Since ancient Mongolian kids don't have video games, they are into a game called *shagai*. It's played with sheep's anklebones. Man, these people are seriously sheep-crazy.

Temujin laughed at the girl's offer. "You only win because you cheat," he said.

"You *wish*," she said and walked off, tossing the sheep-ankle dice.

"That's Borte, my best friend," Temujin told us. "She can be incredibly annoying."

By this time, Sam was about to burst. "*The Book*," he said. "You said you remembered seeing it."

"Oh," said Temujin. "I forget where now."

It looked like we were headed for a long night in Outer Mongolia.

CHAPTER 6

A hush fell over the victory feast as Temujin's father stood up to make a speech. Yesugei raised his goblet in triumph, and addressed the large crowd. "Today," he said, "our warriors achieved a great victory in the field of battle, driving the Tartars from our land."

The crowd went nuts. When they settled down again, Yesugei continued, "I thank the Eternal Blue Heaven for strengthening our swords. And also my *anda*, my blood brother, Toghril, for the courage of his troops."

Another chieftain stood, and T.J.'s dad gave him a big hug. The crowd went crazy again.

Then Yesugei made another announcement. "It is fitting that we mark the end of our struggle with a new beginning. And so I commemorate our victory by declaring that my son and heir, Temujin, and the princess Borte are engaged to be married." The crowd really went bonkers this time.

Fred, Sam, and I could hardly believe our ears. Fred dropped his goblet, and I nearly coughed up my koumiss.

"What?" Sam cried.

"Married?" Fred said. "To a girl? B–but you're our age."

T.J. looked a little embarrassed, but also a little happy. Meanwhile, Borte was beaming from across the room. Temujin's pops seemed pretty excited, too. All of his pals were busy congratulating him and making toasts. Servants refilled goblets as quickly as the men drank.

Fred, Sam, and I were still shocked by the news, so T.J. tried to explain. "Our parents arranged it. But the wedding is still *years* away." Then he added, "And only if she quits cheating at *shagai*."

Fred patted T.J. on the back. "You poor guy. You must've *really* ticked off your folks. Couldn't they just ground you?"

Before Temujin could reply, a scream pierced through the chatter. The crowd started rushing this way and that. People were yelling and fumbling around. It was total chaos.

"Father!" Temujin shouted.

Yesugei was lying on the ground, motionless. His goblet rolled away from his limp hand. Toghril, Yesugei's chieftain friend, rushed to Temujin. "Do not look!" he said, shielding T.J.'s eyes from the sight.

People in the crowd began to murmur. "Poison," they whispered.

Someone in the tent said, "He has been poisoned . . . but who—?"

"There!" a voice called out. It was Tarkutai, the young warrior who had tried to kill Sam. He was pointing to a servant who was trying to slip out of the yurt. "The servant!" Tarkutai said. "He is a Tartar spy!" At that, Tarkutai's goons wrestled the guy to the ground.

But it was too late for Yesugei. Temujin looked at his dad, and then at the servant. His eyes filled with sadness and anger. He ran out of the yurt.

Fred, Sam, and I chased after T.J. We finally caught up with him outside near some boulders. When he turned to look at us, his eyes flashed with rage.

"THEY WILL PAY!" Temujin yelled. "I must now become chief in my father's place—and I will not stop until every last Tartar is wiped off the face of the earth!"

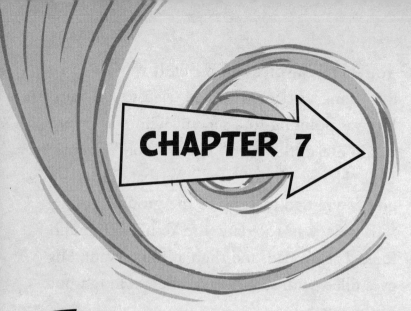

CHAPTER 7

The next day, everyone gathered at the big yurt. Men beat drums slowly, and others did a strange sort of singing—it was like the sounds were coming from their throats, not from their mouths! Today Temujin was becoming the new chieftain.

We tried to get a good spot, but it was kind of tough with all the warriors and nobles crowded into the yurt. Temujin was in the very center of the tent, wearing some fancy clothes and standing on a fancy carpet. Ten old guys were circled around him.

You could tell it was a big deal.

"Man!" Fred exclaimed. "This is *way* cool. I've never had a friend promoted to chieftain before. Though, one of my brothers *did* make hall monitor."

After a while, the singers stopped singing. The drummers kept on with a slow steady beat. The shaman in charge of the ceremony signaled to four servants. Each servant lifted a corner of the carpet Temujin was standing on and lifted him up in the air. T.J. looked pretty tough up there.

Next, the shaman held a big carved staff in front of Temujin. "That's his dad's scepter," Sam whispered. "When the shaman gives it over to T.J., he'll officially be the chieftain." But Sam had spoken too soon. When T.J. reached out to grab the scepter, Tarkutai burst in with his goons, including old Creepy-Eye.

The drumbeat stopped. Everyone looked confused, including the shaman and the servants.

They were so surprised, they dropped the carpet *and* Temujin.

"This travesty must be stopped!" Tarkutai yelled.

"Uh-oh," Fred whispered. "It's Turkey-Toes. What does *he* want?"

The crowd began to murmur. The shaman called out, "Tarkutai, this is sacrilege! Explain yourself!"

Turkey-Toes turned toward the old guys sitting around T.J. "Temujin is a *boy*!" he cried. "In the history of our people, none but a proven warrior—a grown man—has ever been our chieftain."

"What?" Temujin yelled. Like the rest of us, he could hardly believe what a snake Turkey-Toes was being. T.J. drew his scimitar and lunged at

Tarkutai, but Creepy-Eye tripped T.J. before he could reach him. Temujin landed with a thud on the dirt floor.

"Why, that rotten . . . ," Fred muttered. He was staring at Creepy-Eye and getting that dangerous going-to-do-something-crazy look.

"Fred, stay out of it," Sam whispered, grabbing Fred's arm.

Tarkutai pointed at Temujin lying in the dirt. "You see?" he said smugly. "Would *you* follow this *child* into battle?"

That really got T.J. mad. He jumped up and glared right at Turkey-Toes and the old guys. "I am the son of Yesugei, and his rightful heir!" he shouted. "I DEMAND that you finish the ceremony." Then he pointed at Tarkutai and declared, "My first act as royal khan will be to banish you to the Gobi Desert."

Sam's eyes suddenly got big. He tried to get our attention. *"Khan?"* he whispered. "Holy cats. Guys, he's . . ."

"Shh!" I hissed, "I'm trying to hear." Sam was always going on about some little factoid or another at all the wrong times.

By this time, the old guys were starting to look confused—like they might really be buying what Turkey-Toes was telling them.

The shaman finally spoke. "What Tarkutai says has merit, Temujin."

Things were going from bad to worse for T.J., but he wasn't giving up without a fight. "You are traitors!" he said. Then he stared right at Turkey-Toes and roared, "If you wish to hold my father's scepter, you will have to take it from me!" T.J. grabbed the carved scepter from the shaman, who looked a little surprised but didn't try to stop him.

We thought that would shut Turkey-Toes up. But we were wrong. He looked more smug than ever. He gave T.J. a big greasy grin. "Fine," he said. "Then let us settle this the traditional way—*bayirldax*. A wrestling match."

Fred, who'd been pretty quiet for Fred, couldn't hold himself back any longer. He busted through the crowd and marched right up to Tarkutai. "Hold it right there, you big bully!" he shouted. "You're *twice* the size of Temujin."

Fred had a point. T.J. was pretty tough for a nine year old, but Tarkutai was a full-grown adult. Tarkutai wrestling Temujin would be like the Yankees playing my sister, Anna's, T-ball team.

But T.J. was calm. "Fred," he said, laying his hand on Fred's shoulder, "a challenge cannot be refused. But do not worry. I am Borjigin. We *always* win."

Being Borjigin had worked for him on the battlefield, but I had a bad feeling it wasn't going to save T.J. from becoming minced mutton meat in the wrestling ring.

CHAPTER 8

Temujin handed the scepter back to the shaman and took his place opposite Tarkutai.

"Let the match begin," the shaman announced. "The first to fall loses the scepter."

What was supposed to be Temujin's big day had turned into the Saturday Night Super Slapdown. The match was on. Temujin and Tarkutai glared at each other, then bent their knees and spread their arms like two big eagles.

As the drums were beaten, they did some more knee bends and birdlike moves. Finally, they both slapped their thighs as a signal that they were ready to wrestle.

I'd seen wrestling matches on TV before, but never one like this. Fred looked confused, too.

"The goal in Mongolian wrestling," Sam explained, "is to make your opponent touch his back, knee, or elbow to the ground. Each wrestler can get help from a coach on the sidelines, called a *zasuul*, who also sings songs about the wrestler's heroic deeds."

Lucky for T.J., he had three *zasuuls* cheering him on—Fred, Sam, and me. I just hoped when it was all over we'd be singing a victory song. And from the looks of things, I wasn't so sure.

The bird dance was over, and Temujin and Tarkutai were starting to wrestle for real. They locked arms and began to move together in a circle. Tarkutai's leg shot out in a roundhouse kick that almost knocked Temujin off his feet. Luckily, T.J. jumped up just in time. Fred, Sam, and I were cheering from the sidelines.

Annoyed that he didn't land his kick, Tarkutai tried to throw Temujin over his hip. But T.J. did a fancy flip in the air and landed on his feet. As Tarkutai turned to face him, Temujin gave Turkey-Toes a killer head-butt right in his belly.

"*Unh!*" Tarkutai groaned as he staggered backward.

"All right!" *zasuul* Fred cheered. "Now hit him with a power-slam!"

Zasuul Sam and I did our part with our best two-man wave. It looked like T.J. might actually have a chance.

Tarkutai's goons must have been thinking the same thing because Creepy-Eye snuck up through the crowd and pulled a small dagger from his tunic.

Fred saw it first and tried to warn T.J. "Look out!" he cried.

But when T.J. turned, Creepy-Eye angled the dagger so that it reflected sunlight right into his eyes. T.J. stumbled back, blinded. Turkey-Toes moved in like a vulture. He lifted Temujin into the air and slammed him on the ground.

Just like that, it was all over.

CHAPTER 9

*T*emujin lay there, stunned. Tarkutai raised his arms in victory. All his goons cheered. Creepy-Eye smiled an extra-slimy smile.

We rushed over to T.J. and helped him to his feet. "I . . . I don't understand . . . I am Borjigin," he said. You could tell he was really torn up.

"It wasn't you, T.J.," Fred said. "They cheated."

But the truth didn't seem to matter. Tarkutai was already heading toward the shaman to claim the scepter.

"The matter is settled," Tarkutai declared. "*I* will be the new khan." Then he turned to

Temujin and snarled, "And you, little flea, are free to go."

Temujin was still in shock. He looked around at the faces of the people who had once supported him. Then he turned and raced out of the yurt.

Creepy-Eye slipped away after T.J. We made our way through the crowd to follow them. "Wait!" Fred called to T.J. as we headed toward the yurt flap. But suddenly our path was blocked by two of Turkey-Toes's henchmen.

"Move it, yak-breath," said Fred. But these guys clearly weren't taking any orders from Fred.

"Look," said Sam, pointing outside. It was Temujin. He was being dragged away by Creepy-Eye! He was in big trouble. We had to do something.

"Temujin's being yurt-napped!" I yelled at the elders. Two thugs dragged us off to shut us up. But Fred reached out and yanked a rope attached to the yurt.

The yurt walls collapsed like a deflating balloon. In the confusion, the thugs loosened their grip, and Fred, Sam, and I slipped out from under the yurt.

"There he is," said Sam. In the distance T.J. was struggling against Creepy-Eye. We took off running in their direction.

"Uh-oh! We've got company," I said.

Tarkutai's goons were right behind us.

We ducked for cover as arrows whizzed past our ears. The warriors were gaining on us, and there was nowhere to go. A huge flock of sheep was blocking our way. We had to think fast.

"Mutton merge!" I yelled to Sam and Fred, as I dove into the woolly roadblock.

"But my allergy . . . ," Sam protested. A well-aimed arrow whistled past his ear. That changed his mind. Sam joined Fred and me in the pile of sheep.

When the warriors approached, all they saw was your typical Outer Mongolian sheep flock. We had completely pulled the wool over their eyes . . . until Sam let out a huge sneeze.

"Achoooooooo!" echoed through the air, blowing our cover. Sam tried to disguise it with a weak *"Baaaaaaaa!"* But the thugs were on to us. They waded into the flock and cornered three suspicious-looking sheep.

Lucky for us, they picked the wrong puff-balls. We crept up behind the goons and knocked them into the mud.

But we didn't even get to finish our high-fives. The thugs got back on their feet. And now they weren't just armed Mongolian warriors. They were *muddy-and-mad* armed Mongolian warriors.

So much for Plan A. We needed a Plan B. I spied a camel cart nearby. "This way," I called to Sam and Fred. I'd never driven a camel cart before, but this seemed like the perfect time to start.

Fred and Sam crawled into the cart as I jumped onto the surprised camel's back. I took up the reins and gave the camel a kick.

"Yeehaw!" I yelled as the camel took off toward the mountains. I was a real Outer Mongolian cowboy!

We jumped and bounced and rocked our way over some very bumpy ground. I looked over my shoulder to watch Tarkutai's thugs disappearing in the distance.

"Driving one of these is a piece of cake," I said. Which is exactly when the camel decided to make a complete stop.

Sam, Fred, and I flew into a spiny bush.

"Ow," said Fred.

"Oof," I said.

"A real piece of cake," said Sam.

We sat there stunned and aching for a few seconds. "Well, that was fun," said Fred. "Now . . . how are we going to rescue T.J.?"

The fall must have jolted Sam's brain, because he was suddenly dying to tell us something. "Guys, listen," he said. "I figured out who Temujin really is. When he said *khan*, it hit me. He's . . . *Genghis Khan.*"

Then Sam paused and gave Fred and I *the look*—the one where we're supposed to be impressed by something amazing he's just said.

Not getting the reaction he was looking for, Sam plowed on. "Genghis Khan?" he said even more dramatically. "As in, the greatest conqueror of all time? As in, the guy who ruled the largest empire *ever*?"

"Interesting," said Fred, doing his best to humor Sam. "So anyway, how are we going to rescue T.J.?"

Sam smacked his head in disgust, but I was with Fred. This was no time for one of Sam's history lessons. Temujin was in trouble, and we needed a game plan.

"Turkey-Toes's men are all over that camp," I said. "There's no way we can go back without getting killed."

We were just letting this thought sink in when our camel added his thoughts on the subject by spitting a giant green loogie onto my head. The Phlegm Monster had nothing on this guy.

"Eew," said Sam, holding his head.

"Urg," said Fred, grabbing his stomach. I reached up and felt the sticky glob in my hair.

"That gives me a great idea," I said.

CHAPTER 10

Back at the camp, we found the yurt Temujin was being held in. From outside, we could hear his voice.

"You festering wart!" T.J. yelled angrily at someone inside. "Why am I being held? I demand that you release me!"

"Oh, shush," a boy answered back. "You're not going anywhere. Not until Tarkutai decides what to do with you."

It was time for us to make our move.

At this point, I should probably mention that Fred, Sam, and I were dressed like servant-girls.

It was all part of my plan. See, the camel spit made me think of covering my head by wearing a wig . . . which made me think of wearing a disguise . . . which made me think . . . well, whatever. We dressed up like servant-girls to sneak back into camp.

I walked into the yurt carrying a large tray of food. "Suppertime," I said in my best servant-girl voice.

The guy guarding Temujin turned out to be Turkey-Toes's little brother, Pumlik. When he saw us come in, he looked up. "What's going on?" he asked suspiciously.

Fred wasn't too thrilled with the whole dress-like-a-girl thing, but Sam really got into character. "We're traveling caterers," Sam said in a high-pitched voice. "We're bringing you a nice heaping plate of 'I Can't Believe It's Not Mutton.'"

"I hate mutton," Pumlik griped. "I want some bordzig."

"I'm so sorry," Fred said. "Somebody must have messed up your order."

Pumlik gave Fred the once-over. "Hey, you're cute." he said. "What's your name?"

"What's it to you, ya big . . ." Fred grumbled in a very un-girlish voice.

But Sam interrupted before Pumlik got suspicious. "I'm . . . er . . . Shashlick," Sam blurted, then motioned to Fred and me. "And these are my sisters, Saltlick and Cowlick."

Pumlik smiled smugly and said, "My brother is the new khan. So . . . which one of you gets to be my girlfriend?" Then he gave Fred a wink.

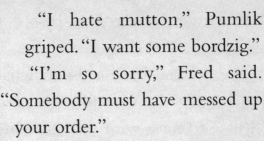

"Want to meet me later by the sheep-dung pile?"

Fred pulled back a fist to whack Pumlik, but I grabbed him before he got the chance. "I hate to mess with your love life, Cowlick, but aren't you forgetting something?" I said, giving Fred the eye.

Fred got the hint. He gritted his teeth and put on his best girl voice. "Would you mind holding the drink tray while I pour?" he squeaked to Pumlik.

"For you? Anything," Pumlik said, wiggling his eyebrows at Fred.

"Uh, and if you could just hold onto my food tray, too, while I serve," I added.

"But of course," Pumlik said, grinning like a goofball.

Once both trays were in Pumlik's hands, we let him have it. Fred and I clanged the trays on either side of Pumlik's head like a giant set of cymbals.

Pumlik fell to the ground in a dizzy heap.

We rushed over to T.J. and started untying the ropes that bound him.

"Hurry," said Sam.

"T.J., listen," Fred said quickly. "That wrestling match—Turkey-Toes cheated. His goon pulled a knife and blinded you."

"What?" said Temujin.

"It's true," I said. "Which means you're the real khan!"

Pumlik was starting to come around. Temujin clonked him back to dreamland.

"Come on, guys," said Sam. "Let's go."

"No. I cannot," Temujin said firmly.

"What?" Sam, Fred, and I shouted at the same time.

"Tarkutai is planning to announce his engagement to Borte," T.J. explained. "I must stay and rescue her."

"That's crazy," Sam said. "Once Tarkutai's men spot you, you'll be dead mutton."

"You're right," T.J. said with a grin. "But I have an idea."

CHAPTER 11

T.J.'s idea may not have been inspired by a camel loogie, but the result was the same. Somehow Sam, Fred, and I were still dressed like girls. This time we found ourselves behind a boulder by a stream near camp.

"You know what?" Fred said, looking grumpier than ever. "His ideas are even worse than yours."

"Quit griping," I whispered. "Hey, there's Borte."

Borte was with a group of girls on their way to the stream. They all had water jugs balanced on their heads. Borte was at the end of the line, and there was a huge guy walking beside her.

"They've got a guard on her," Sam said.

We had to find a way to sneak past the guard and get to Borte. I spotted three empty water jugs . . . and had an idea.

Sam, Fred, and I grabbed the jugs and put them on our heads. As the girls made their way past the boulder we were hiding behind, we fell into line behind Borte.

"*Psst.* Borte," I whispered.

Borte looked startled. "Who are you?" she asked suspiciously.

"We're friends of Temujin," I said. "We've come to rescue you."

"And we are not girls," Fred added.

"Riiiiight," Borte said, slowly beginning to recognize us. "Where's Temujin?"

"Temujin's waiting for you in the forest," I said. "As soon as we rescue you, he's going to declare war on Tarkutai."

"Great," Borte said. "So what's the plan?"

"That is a very good question," said Sam.

"Maybe if we spit on Joe's head we'll get an idea," Fred suggested.

Borte gave us a strange look.

We'd finally reached the stream, and the girls had begun to fill up their water jugs. We only had a few minutes. It was the only plan I could think of. I pushed Sam into the stream.

"He-ey," he spluttered. He began thrashing around in the water like a drowning duck.

"Help! Help!" I squealed in a high-pitched voice. "My sister is drowning!"

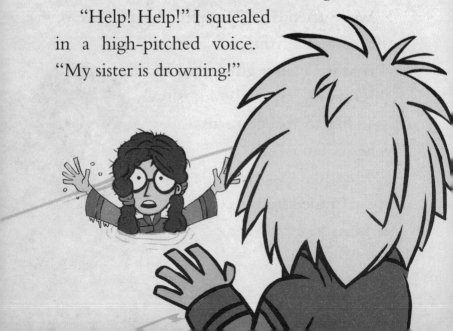

The plan worked. Borte's bodyguard quickly jumped into the stream to save Sam. Now Borte could slip away unseen.

"Take Borte to Temujin," I told Fred. "Go." I had to stay behind and save Sam . . . from being saved.

The bodyguard grabbed at the back of Sam's headdress.

"Stop," Sam said. But it was too late. Sam's headdress—and disguise—came off in the guard's hand.

The bodyguard narrowed his eyes and hauled Sam out of the water. But before he could pulverize Sam, I shoved my own headdress down over his eyes.

"Wha—?" the bodyguard grunted, dropping Sam to the ground.

Sam and I made a new plan to run for the woods as fast as our skirted legs would carry us.

We made it to the clearing in the woods where Fred, Borte, and T.J. were waiting with fresh horses. Sam, Fred, and I gladly changed out of our Mongolian servant-girl costumes.

"Thank you for coming to my rescue," Borte said.

"Well, next time I'll be wearing pants," said Fred.

Temujin gave us all a serious look. "Now it's my turn. I must deal with Tarkutai," he said, as he made a move toward one of the horses.

T.J. was ready to teach Turkey-Toes a lesson, but if he acted too hastily it could be a disaster.

"Wait," said Sam. "You can't beat Tarkutai all by yourself."

"Of course I can!" Temujin roared. "I am Borjigin! And he is a groveling worm!"

Oh, no. Not this "I am Borjigin" business again. It was time to talk some sense into T.J.

"Tarkutai's got all those goons with him," I reminded Temujin. Then I had yet another great idea. "Remember at the feast," I said. "That old friend of your dad's . . . wasn't he chief of some tribe or another?"

Temujin thought for a minute. Then a huge smile spread across his face.

In no time, we were at Chief Toghril's yurt. We stood behind T.J. as he explained the whole story to his dad's friend.

"And so it is," Temujin said, "that the legacy of my father, your blood brother, has been stolen from me. I ask only for help in righting what is wrong."

When Temujin finished, Toghril replied without hesitation. "You may have whatever you need—men, horses, weapons. Your father was my closest friend."

Temujin bowed his head. "Thank you," he said. "I will prepare now for battle."

T.J. turned to go, but Sam pulled him back.

"Wait," Sam said, addressing Temujin and Toghril. "One more thing. We're looking for a book: It's blue, with squiggles on it."

"Book?" Toghril replied, looking confused. "I don't know this word."

"Oh, yes," T.J. said, thinking of our earlier descriptions. "Their 'book' is square, like a box. I know I have seen it, but I just can't remember . . ."

"Perhaps you mean the strange blue object the shaman found," Toghril suggested.

"The shaman," T.J. said, slapping his forehead. "*That* is where I saw it."

"Great," Sam said. "Now we're getting somewhere."

"It was to be a gift for the new khan," T.J. explained. "Which means . . . Tarkutai has it."

Fred, Sam, and I moaned together like Mongolian throat-singers, "Oh, *maaaaaan . . .*"

CHAPTER 12

Now Temujin had men and horses, but he still had to prove himself as a warrior. T.J. rode bravely to the front of his new army. Behind their leader, the warriors waved their weapons and let out a series of battle cries.

Turkey-Toes was in for some trouble and—without *The Book*—it looked like we were going along for the ride. Fred, Sam, Borte, and I brought up the rear of the pack as we charged toward camp.

When we reached camp, Tarkutai looked like he'd seen a ghost.

"It's Temujin!" he said to Creepy-Eye, as he leaped onto his horse. "Quickly! Find my men! Archers to the front! Show no mercy!"

In no time, the battle had begun. Tarkutai may have been caught off guard, but he wasn't going down without a fight.

As the fight heated up, Sam, Fred, and I took the opportunity to look for *The Book*, with Borte's help.

"There," she said pointing ahead of us. "That's Tarkutai's yurt." Since the shaman would have given *The Book* to Tarkutai, there was a good chance we'd find it in his quarters.

We hurried inside and began turning the place inside out. "It's gotta be in here somewhere," I said. "Borte, keep a lookout."

We threw aside carpets and clothes and cushions, but didn't see anything that looked like *The Book*.

"Nothing." Sam groaned. "It's not here."

"It's got to be," I said. "Keep looking."

Fred picked up a brass pitcher and threw it onto a pile of carpets nearby. "Ow!" the pile yelled.

Fred pulled back the talking carpets.

"Pumlik!" we all yelled.

"Hey," Pumlik whined, digging back into the pile. "Go find your own hiding place."

"Pumlik," said Borte, "this is really important. Please help us."

"We're looking for a blue 'box' with silver designs on it," I explained to him. "Can you tell us where it is?"

"Never," Pumlik huffed. "Not even if you torture me."

Fred took this as an invitation. He grabbed Pumlik by the collar and gave him a fierce glare.

Pumlik grumbled.

"Tarkutai's got it," he squealed. "It's in his saddlebag."

Then Pumlik looked back at Fred. "Don't I know you?" he asked. "You have beautiful eyes."

Fred tossed Pumlik back onto the pile of carpets, and we all set off to find Tarkutai.

Back on the battlefield, things were looking bad for Temujin. Tarkutai's men were chasing down T.J. and his troops, who were making a speedy retreat. *How could this be happening?*

Then suddenly, Toghril's men, the Kereit warriors, appeared on all sides. Tarkutai's men were surrounded. Temujin wasn't retreating after all. He'd just set a trap, and Tarkutai had fallen right into it.

Tarkutai and his men stumbled this way and that on their horses, searching for an escape. The Kereit soldiers closed in on them. Tarkutai was locked in combat with one of the warriors—a dagger was gripped in his teeth and his scimitar sliced through the air. We could see a corner of *The Book* peeking out of his saddlebag.

"Great," Sam moaned. "Now we'll never get it."

"Hey, look," said Fred. "Turkey-Toes's men are taking off."

Fred was right. Tarkutai's gang of supporters was heading for the hills.

"Temujin is winning!" Borte cried.

Tarkutai seemed to notice this, too.

All of sudden, he pulled a U-turn with his horse and headed for the hills himself.

"*Woo-hoo!*" Fred cheered. "Look at Turkey-Toes go."

"*Aaagh!*" Sam screamed. "*Turkey-Toes is going—with* The Book*!*"

In an instant, Fred jumped on the back of the nearest horse, and landed with a thud.

"What are you doing?" I yelled.

"It's now or never, right?" Fred exclaimed. "Giddy-up!"

With that, he gave the horse a swift kick and took off after Tarkutai. Fred's horse bounced along wildly, and then it reared up on its back legs, nearly sending Fred sailing.

"No! Down! Reverse!" Fred commanded his horse.

Somehow Fred caught up to Tarkutai. Sweeping in from behind, Fred snatched *The Book* from the Mongol's saddlebag.

Tarkutai glared over his shoulder. Fred held up *The Book* and gave Tarkutai a sly grin and a little wave. *That was probably not a good idea.* In a flash, Tarkutai was swinging at Fred with his scimitar.

Fred took the hint and turned his horse to flee, but now Turkey-Toes was hot on his tail, scimitar flashing.

It looked like curtains for Fred, but T.J. came flying to the rescue.

"Tarkutai!" Temujin yelled, heading straight for Turkey-Toes at a full gallop. T.J. had a score to settle, and he was going to do it man-to-man.

Fred came bouncing back to Sam, Borte, and I, waving *The Book*.

"YEE-HAW!" he howled. "I got it!"

Fred was so excited, he didn't notice Creepy-Eye racing up on his horse behind him. "Fred! Behind you!" I yelled.

He turned around just in time. Creepy-Eye slashed his dagger and missed. Fred whacked Creepy-Eye with *The Book*, sending him flying off his horse. In one swift movement, Fred lifted one leg over Creepy-Eye's horse and rode toward us smiling. Apparently he *could* ride two horses at once.

"This book really is a lifesaver," said Fred. He pulled his horses to a stop and slid off.

Green wisps of smoke curled out of *The Book*.

Just then, T.J. rode up on his horse.

"The battle is ours," he said. "Tarkutai has been vanquished."

Borte beamed up at him. "You're truly worthy of becoming khan," she said proudly.

The green time-warping mist circled around us.

"Uh-oh," I announced. "Looks like our ride's here."

T.J. turned to face Fred, Sam, and I. "Thank you for your help, my friends," he said. "Oh, and Fred—before I forget—"

But we were already gone.

CHAPTER 13

Back in my kitchen, we carefully opened *The Book.* There, on the page, a tiny T.J. smiled back. "I've been practicing," he said. Then he gave us one killer armpit fart.

"I taught him that, you know," Fred said.

I closed *The Book* as Sam began gathering the trading cards that had scattered all over the floor when we time-warped.

"I wonder why they don't make Genghis Khan cards," Sam said, holding up the Phlegm Monster card. "He's *much* more interesting than this guy."

"I'm not saying you're wrong," Fred replied. "But don't deny the Phlegm, okay?"

"So . . . anyone up for this Mongolian barbeque?" I asked. All that time traveling had made me hungry. "They've got a mutton platter," I added, after giving the menu the once-over.

"What *is* mutton anyway?" Fred asked suspiciously.

"Old sheep," Sam replied.

We'd all had just about enough sheep to last a lifetime. I tossed the menu aside. "I've got peanut butter and jelly right here," I suggested.

Sam and Fred smiled. "That works," they said.

"Hey, Sam," I said. "You know what goes great with peanut butter and jelly?"

"What?" Sam asked.

I smiled. "An ice-cold glass of koumiss."